Hero of the Land of Snow

Hero of the Land of Snow

Adapted by Sylvia Gretchen from

the Tibetan Epic Tale of Gesar

Illustrated by Julia Witwer

DHARMA  PUBLISHING

Library of Congress Cataloging-in-Publication Data

Gretchen, Sylvia.
  Hero of the land of snow.

  Summary: Recounts the Tibetan myth about the magical
birth and heroic exploits of young Gesar.
  1. Gesar (Legendary character)--Juvenile literature.
2. Mythology, Tibetan--Juvenile literature [1. Gesar
(Legendary character) 2. Mythology, Tibetan] I. Witwer,
Julia, ill. II. Gesar. English. III. Title.
BL1950.T5G74 1990   398.22′0951′5   89−25603
ISBN 0−89800−201−X
ISBN 0−89800−202−8 (pbk.)

Printed in the USA by Dharma Press

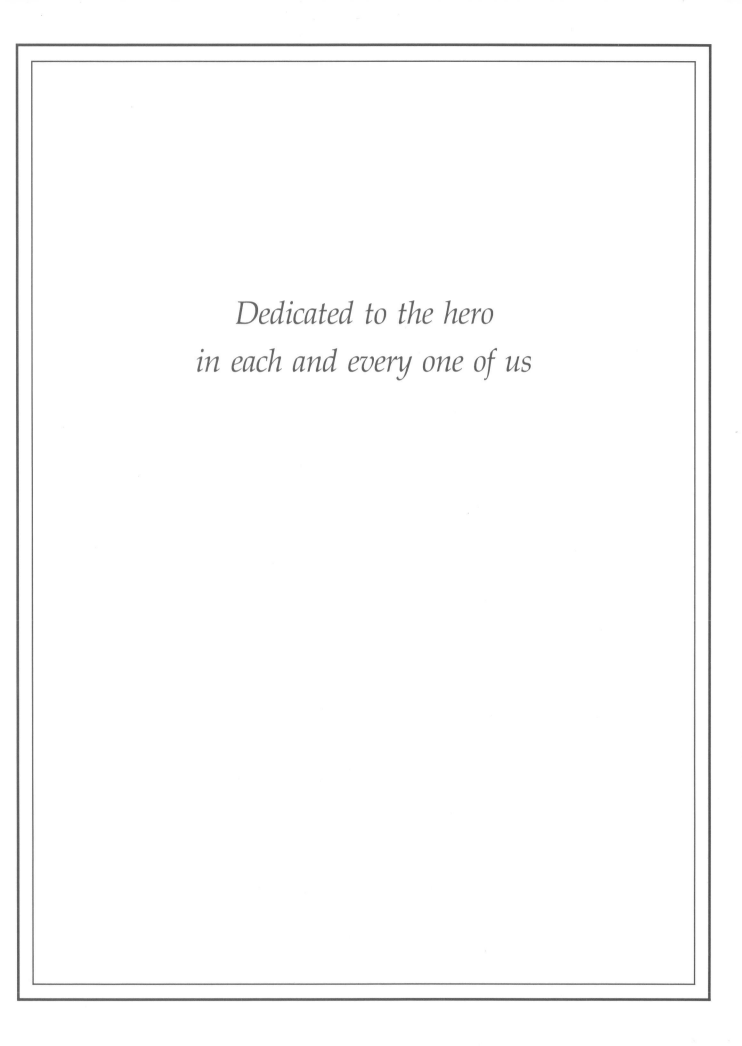

*Dedicated to the hero
in each and every one of us*

Mother, I am Gesar, the Lion King.

Long ago in the snowy land of Ling, high in the mountains of Tibet, the magical Gesar was born. A hero destined for great endeavors and adventures, Gesar was sent to earth to defend all that is good and to vanquish evil.

At the time of Gesar's birth rainbows arched from the high peaks, across the green fields and flowing rivers of Ling to touch the little home where his mother, Gogmo, held him in her arms. Opening clear, bright eyes, the newborn Gesar smiled and said, "Mother, I am Gesar, the Lion King."

Many years ago, the old king of Ling had left on a pilgrimage. When he did not return, rich and powerful lords divided the land. Some ruled wisely. But others, led by the evil Lord Trotun, plundered the land and oppressed the people. Year by year Trotun's power increased, and so did the misery of the people of Ling.

According to an ancient prophecy, a magical child would one day become the greatest king that Ling had ever known. Gesar had the power of speech from birth, and in one week he grew as a normal child would in one month. Fearing that Lord Trotun and his men would harm Gesar, Gogmo tried to keep her wondrous son out of sight. But little Gesar, full of mischief and magic, would have none of his mother's protection, and soon found ways to escape from his home.

"Gone again!" exclaimed Gogmo, rushing out of the house. "Where can he be this time? In the market begging for fruit, or in the streets teasing the horsemen?" When she found him and began to scold him for his mischief, Gesar smiled at his mother and sang her a riddle:

"When the lion roars, the fox trembles in his den.
When the eagle flies, the sparrows hide in the trees.

When Gesar walks, evil flies away.
Gesar sees the heart and knows the mind.
He has no fear of humankind."

One day Gesar was racing on a stick horse with a group of small boys. A horseman rode by, commanding, "Clear the road, for the great Lord Trotun comes!" Quickly the children scrambled to the side of the road, all but Gesar, who remained to face Lord Trotun and his mounted warriors. Trotun's face twisted in an angry scowl when he saw the boy in his path. "Do you know who I am?" he bellowed.

"Of course! Trotun," Gesar replied, "I know who you are, but do you know who I am?"

Lord Trotun's scowl deepened. "Throw him aside," he commanded his warriors. Yet try as they might, Trotun's men could not even dismount, and their horses would not move forward. They cracked their whips and dug in their spurs, but Gesar's magic held them fast.

Laughter began to ripple through the crowd that was gathering to watch the great Trotun and his warriors helpless before a child. Trotun's pasty face flushed and his fat body began to shake with rage. Finally Gesar stepped aside, saying, "Now you shall remember me, Trotun. I am Gesar, and I will be your master and your king."

Instantly Trotun's horse leapt forward, Trotun desperately clinging to the saddle. "So that is Gesar," thought Trotun. He had heard strange stories about Gesar, and now he remembered a prophecy that a magical child would become a mighty king.

"I must be rid of him!" Trotun cried out.

But Trotun was a coward, and feared the child's magical power. So the next day he sought out the most cruel sorcerer in the land, a fearsome-looking man called Ratna the Evil, and offered him gold and jewels to destroy Gesar.

The greedy sorcerer retired to his dark cave and prepared his powerful spells. Then, striding to the mouth of his cave, Ratna the Evil hurled fiery lightning bolts to strike Gesar as he played in the fields. Gesar raised his hand like a shield, sending the lightning flashing back to land at Ratna the Evil's feet.

Angered that his magic spell had failed, Ratna the Evil commanded three monstrous birds with razor-sharp talons and beaks like knives to attack the boy. Seeing the birds in pursuit, Gesar took up his toy bow and loosed three stick arrows. The arrows pierced their hearts and the huge birds shattered into one hundred black shapes that disappeared like wisps of clouds into the clear blue sky.

When his magical birds did not return, Ratna the Evil went to the mountain peak to look for them. Seeing Gesar gathering herbs in the valley below, Ratna lifted a boulder larger than a man and sent it thundering right into Gesar's path. Looking towards the peak where the sorcerer stood, Gesar laughed and batted the boulder away as a child might bat away a ball.

Returning to Lord Trotun, Ratna the Evil was forced to admit defeat: "This child's magic is the greatest I have ever seen. I fear for my own life if I continue to challenge him." Turning his back on Lord Trotun, Ratna the Evil went back to his cave.

Infuriated, Trotun came up with another scheme to rid himself of Gesar. Calling for a meeting of the nobles of the land, he charged that Gesar was an evil spirit who would bring harm to the people if he remained in Ling. For the kingdom's safety, Gesar must be sent into the northern desert far from any town or village.

Afraid to go against Lord Trotun's will, the nobles quickly agreed. There were those among them who had watched Gesar's progress with great interest, hoping that one day he would challenge Trotun's power. If he were the prophesied king, they knew he would be protected even in the North. "When the time is right," they thought, "Gesar will return to Ling."

In this way Gogmo and Gesar were forced to leave the beautiful valley of Ling. Hundreds lined the streets as they left, many with tears in their eyes and prayers in their hearts for Gesar's safe return.

Gesar led his mother's horse, singing as he walked. "Don't be afraid. Groundhogs will serve us, vultures will tell us news. We shall feast on juicy roots and watch the blue sky for amusement. I leave to tame the northern wastes, for wherever Gesar goes he has a task to fulfill!"

For many days, Gesar and Gogmo traveled through the treacherous mountains that led to the northern desert. At first they met other travelers and passed encampments of nomads tending their herds. Then they came to a land where no men lived and few men ventured, a wild and desolate land of sudden storms and hidden dangers.

Gesar led his mother to the edge of a broad plain. "Look there, Mother! Can you not see our new home?"

"Son, I see nothing but rocks and sand and scrubby plants. I see no food and no water and not a living soul. Have you brought us to ruin with your magic and mischief?"

Gesar led his mother's horse through the treacherous mountains.

But there, in the shelter of a small hill, a tiny spring bubbled forth crystal pure water. Nearby, Gesar and Gogmo built a small hut that would keep away the cold winter wind and the harsh summer sun.

Gesar spent his days exploring, running with the deer and playing with the shy groundhogs that lived in cozy holes in the sandy earth. When he returned at dusk he would always bring some roots or berries which his mother fashioned into tasty meals.

By night Gesar used his magical powers of transformation to challenge the ghost-like monsters that inhabited the North. It was they who caused the sudden storms and rockfalls that bedeviled man and beast alike. Gradually, Gesar brought these powerful creatures under control, forcing them to swear oaths to help, not harm, living beings.

While Gesar was in exile in the desert, a very special girl named Brougmo was growing up in Ling. Everyone who saw Brougmo agreed that she was the most beautiful girl born in Ling for one hundred generations. Her hair glistened, her eyes sparkled, and her smile shone like the sun. Everything about her glowed with loveliness and kindness. It was as though a goddess had appeared on earth. By the time she turned sixteen there was not a single man in Ling who did not hope that she would become his bride.

Gesar had never met Brougmo, but he knew of her. For as the prophecy said: "The King of Ling shall have as queen one who shines and sparkles like light. He shall also ride a horse that runs with the wind and speaks with a human voice."

One night, a heavenly being appeared to Gesar in a dream, saying, "Gesar, your work here is finished. If you do not return to

Ling soon, your destined queen and your magical horse will be lost to you, and you may never be king."

Although Gesar could have used his magical powers to return to defeat Lord Trotun, he knew that a true king ruled through the loyalty and love of his people, not through magic or force. Slowly a plan began to form in his mind, one that would need the help of Gogmo, the lovely Brougmo, and even the evil Trotun.

That night, Gesar transformed himself into a huge raven and flew to Ling. Entering Trotun's dimly lit tent, he woke him with these words: "Noble Trotun! I bear a message from the gods! Tomorrow you must arrange a meeting of all the lords of Ling. Tell them that the old king has passed to the heavenly realms. A great horse race must be held whose winner will become the undisputed ruler of Ling. He will marry the beautiful Brougmo, and will receive all the treasures of the land.

"Every man of Ling, from the highest lord to the lowest beggar, must be invited to the race. Even the scoundrel Gesar, if he still lives, must be allowed to vie for the crown. Then no man may dispute the winner's claim to the throne.

"Lord Trotun, the gods have decreed that you will be the winner! Your mighty horse will easily defeat all others!"

Trotun's greed and vanity made him believe every word the raven said. Bowing to the raven, Trotun held out a magnificent sky-blue turquoise and promised to do what the raven asked. With a nod, the raven grasped the turquoise in his claw, flapped his mighty wings, and disappeared from sight.

Trotun couldn't sleep. How fitting that he had been chosen as

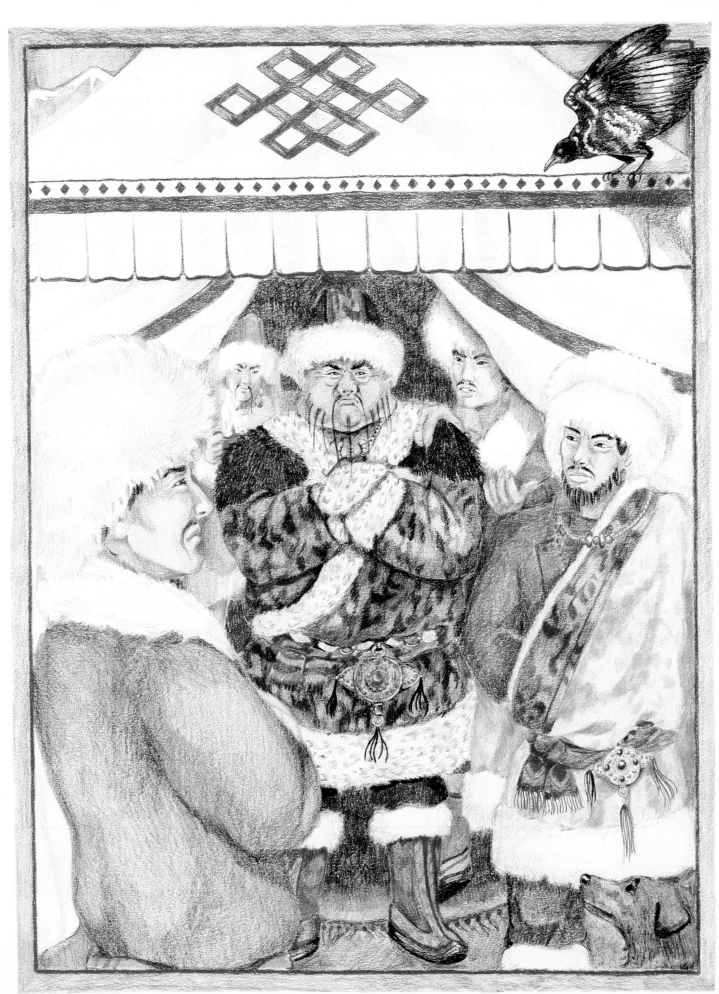

Lord Trotun summoned the nobles of Ling to a great council.

king! Soon he would clasp the lovely Brougmo in his arms and possess all the treasure of Ling! With the first rays of dawn he sent messengers to the lords of Ling, summoning a grand council.

With honeyed tongue, Trotun relayed the message from the marvelous raven, but did not reveal that he, Trotun, was the sure winner of the race.

The wise and gentle Lord Chipon rose up and spoke, "Trotun, whether you were visited by the gods, I know not, but it is time that we ended our disputes and jealousies and chose a king. A race will give us a king and bring peace to our land. Brougmo will make a fine queen, but she is young and untested. Let us give her the chance to prove her worth by carrying news of the race to Gesar. And let the best man in Ling cross the finish line first!"

The lords agreed with Chipon that a great race should be held for the throne and treasures of Ling. A race course was set through the hills and valleys of Ling that would test the strength of the finest rider. The young Lord Changpa was sent to tell Brougmo that she would be queen and that she must find Gesar and bring him to the race.

That same night a strange dream had come to Brougmo. A magnificent rainbow arose in the sky. When it touched the earth a handsome young man appeared from its midst. He spoke the words, "I am King Gesar," and at once, flowers burst into bloom around him, and birds began to sing.

As the evening sun was setting, Lord Changpa found Broug-mo standing alone beside her parent's tent. "Brougmo, you have been greatly honored. The council of nobles has chosen you as Queen of Ling. Your king will be the victor of a great race. Yet, before the race can be run, it has been decreed that you must go alone to the northern desert and return with Gesar if he still lives."

"Go to the northern desert!" Brougmo exclaimed. "And then become Queen of Ling! What of my life here, my family and friends?" Then she remembered the man she had seen in her dream and all fear and hesitation left her.

Determined to find the Gesar of her dream, Brougmo packed food for four weeks of travel as Changpa had instructed. The next morning she said goodbye to her family and set out alone through the same ravines and canyons that Gesar and his mother had entered so long ago.

By day she rode through the desolate landscape, calling Gesar's name. At night she spread her blanket on the rough ground to sleep. After two weeks she came to the edge of a broad plain. In the distance she saw a lone figure. Brougmo's heart leapt with joy as she came closer and made out the form of a young man. Standing with his back to her, he was staring intently at seven groundhogs running in circles before him. "Gesar!" Broug-mo called. "Is it you?"

Without turning, Gesar replied, "Yes, Gesar is what they call me. But who are you, a girl dressed in silks and jewels, come to the middle of the desert to disturb my play?"

"Gesar, I am Brougmo of Ling. I have come to give you important news. There is to be a great race whose winner will become the King of Ling. I am also a prize of this race, for the winner will have my hand in marriage. Please, you must return to Ling and ride in the race. I don't know who you really are, but Gesar, I hope you win."

Brougmo blushed deeply at her bold words. Gesar laughed as

You must go to the northern desert and tell Gesar of the race.

I've ridden all over this desolate land looking for you.

he turned to face Brougmo. Even dressed in rags, his hair unkempt, Gesar's face was strong and handsome. His clear eyes penetrated right to her heart. Taking Brougmo's hand he said, "How can I ride in a great race? I have only a stick horse with neither saddle nor bridle, and these are my very best clothes. Besides, I am happy here with my little friends."

He paused, then continued in a gentler tone. "Well, I do know a wonderful horse. He roams somewhere between here and heaven. He won't come to me. He says I've neglected him too long. I also have a bridle, saddle, and armor, but they are locked in a crystal cave, and I can't go in. So, Brougmo, if you'd like me to return to Ling, you must catch my horse and fetch my saddle."

Sudden anger flashed in Brougmo's eyes. "Gesar, I've ridden all over this desolate land for weeks looking for you, calling your name. I prayed to find you alive, to find the Gesar that I saw in my dream. Now I see that you are a lazy scoundrel who'd rather race groundhogs than race to be my husband and king. You can get your own horse and saddle. I'm pretty enough to find some other prince!"

"Brougmo," Gesar said softly, "your beauty is a fine thing but it will not make you a queen." He tapped Brougmo on the shoulder and instantly her beautiful clothes began to fray and tatter. In horror she reached for her hair and felt it shorn and ragged. Touching her skin she felt it rough and loose.

In the midst of Brougmo's panic, her eyes met Gesar's untroubled gaze. Suddenly she understood the lesson that Gesar was teaching her: her pride in her beauty was foolish! Her youth would fade, one day she would be old. Only her deeds and the goodness of her heart truly mattered.

"Gesar," she said, "I will find your horse and your saddle, and ride beside you to Ling if you will have me."

"Thank you, Brougmo," Gesar said gently. "I need your help." With these words Brougmo's skin once again became soft and smooth, her hair long and lustrous, and her clothes bright and lovely. If anything, she was more beautiful than before, for not the slightest trace of pride remained.

Taking Brougmo's hand, Gesar led her to his small house where Gogmo had just finished preparing the evening meal. On rough clay plates Gogmo served a simple but delicious stew of roots and herbs. As they ate Gesar described the wondrous horse.

"His name is Kyanshay, the 'All-Knowing One'. He is no ordinary horse. His coat, glossy as spring water, is ruby red; his ears resemble eagle feathers; his blue-black mane and tail, like banners of silk, billow out behind him as he runs. He is blessed with the power of flight, the wisdom of language, and the heart of compassion.

"At this moment Kyanshay frolics with one hundred stallions and one hundred mares not far from here. You will need Gogmo's help to catch and tame this horse; he has a mind of his own. Go to him soon or I fear that he will leave us forever."

Gesar appeared as a mighty warrior on the summit of a mountain.

Early the next morning Brougmo and Gogmo set off for the distant meadows. There they watched a herd of horses move gracefully over a ridge and settle down to graze in a grassy valley. In the midst of the group of horses, Brougmo spied Kyanshay, his red coat glistening in the sunlight, his hooves barely touching the earth as he pranced among the herd.

"Kyanshay, come," Brougmo called out. "I have a fine bridle for you and a noble master to serve."

Kyanshay raised his head at her words, and replied in clear tones. "Gesar has already failed to tame me. He will have to find some other steed. I have been wild too long to accept a master."

"It is Brougmo who calls you, not Gesar," said Brougmo. "I have grain and sugar. I will sing you a song about Gesar's adventures with his wondrous horse Kyanshay!"

Brougmo sang in a voice so beguiling and soft that Kyanshay stood entranced, not noticing Gogmo move slowly to his side. With a single motion, Gogmo slipped a lasso over his head and jumped upon his back.

Kyanshay leapt straight into the sky, carrying Gogmo with him. Now Gogmo sang gently to the horse as he galloped wildly through the clouds, telling him of the fine stable he would have in Ling, and of his great master's need for his service. Little by little Kyanshay grew calm, but he still would not return to earth. Finally Gesar, the master magician, appeared as a mighty warrior on the summit of a mountain. Pointing at Kyanshay, he raised his whip and commanded him in a mighty voice to return to earth.

With a single bound the magnificent horse returned to Brougmo. Now docile, he took the sugar and grain Brougmo offered as she and Gogmo joyfully led him to Gesar.

Gesar smiled as Kyanshay nuzzled his hand but said not a word of thanks. Turning to Brougmo with twinkling eyes he asked, "Now what shall I do with this horse since I have no saddle for him? How can I ride with the heroes of Ling without armor?"

"Oh Gesar, tell me the way to the crystal cave so I can get your saddle and armor. Then please ride Kyanshay to Ling and win the great race."

"You do not need directions," replied Gesar. "Once you start searching you will find the cave, just as you found me."

The next day Brougmo set out for the crystal cave. At first she was uncertain of the way. But the further she went into the hills, the firmer her steps became. Halfway up the side of a stony outcropping her attention was drawn to a small deer who seemed to disappear into the mountain itself. When she reached the place where she had last seen the deer, she spied an opening the size of a man. Stepping inside a cave she saw a soft glow coming from a long passage. As she walked down the passage the rough gray stone walls became streaked with clear crystal and finally gave way to a chamber whose crystal walls glowed with a soft white light. There before her stood the deer. As she approached in wonder, the deer changed into the most beautiful woman she had ever seen.

"Brougmo, I am the guardian of the treasures that you are now worthy to receive. Give them to Gesar so that he may accomplish his appointed tasks."

As suddenly as the goddess had appeared, she was gone. Where she had been standing Brougmo saw a finely worked saddle, a rich woolen blanket, a golden bridle, and a magnificent suit of armor.

Gesar placed the golden armor on his shoulders.

She gathered these up in her arms, wondering how she could possibly carry them all the way to Gesar's hut. Then she heard Gesar's familiar voice calling from the entrance of the cave:

"Come, Brougmo, it is not such a long way."

With difficulty she lifted the armor and saddle over her shoulders and stumbled to the entrance of the cave. She was overjoyed to find Gesar and Kyanshay waiting there for her.

Gently, Gesar lifted the bridle, saddle, and armor from her shoulders. "You have shown great courage," he said.

As Gesar placed the golden armor on his shoulders all trace of the beggar she had first seen playing in the desert was gone. Before her stood a king, clearly able to command an army of thousands and rule a country with wisdom and compassion.

"Brougmo, it is good that you see my true form. But it is not yet time for me to cast off my beggar's disguise entirely. Others too must be tested. If the lords of Ling can also see my true nature though I am dressed as a beggar, then I will accomplish much as king and Ling will be renowned far and wide.

"You should now return to Ling. Let it be known that you have found the beggar Gesar and that he lags behind on his pony."

Brougmo left Gesar reluctantly. Making her way quickly back to Ling, she said only that she had found Gesar and that he would come in time for the race. But all who saw and spoke to her wondered at the change in Brougmo; her radiant smile and kindly actions had not changed, but her eyes shone with a new courage and joy.

The day of the race dawned clear and bright. Flags marked the course of the race. The route began on the hill named Avi at the edge of the valley of Ling, then led into the mountains, through ravines, and then circled out into the valley again to the finish line.

The air crackled with excitement as the racers assembled. Banners blew in the brisk breezes; tents, placed on sunny slopes near the finish line, ruffled in the wind. All of Ling had come to see the race. The lords arrived in brilliant robes of yellow, white, and blue. Their horses were adorned with gold and silver, saddles hung with bells, with pennants streaming in the wind. The crowd cheered as each magnificent lord passed by. The horses pranced with excitement, while their riders reined them in, aware of the admiring glances of the lovely ladies in silks and jewels gathered at the starting line.

Lord Trotun was the grandest of all. Certain that he would be king before the day was over, he had indulged in the most expensive silks and furs to cover his fat body. It would have been impossible to find a place for one more piece of silver or one more strip of braid on his clothes or horse. He gazed arrogantly at the crowd, already counting his wealth and leering at the lovely Brougmo.

Brougmo stood atop a small hill beside the golden throne that had been placed for the winner. Anxiously, she watched for Gesar, who appeared only minutes before the race was to start.

"Here is Gesar, our beggar king, riding a nag and carrying his famous stick horse!" someone called from the crowd. And indeed Gesar resembled a beggar in every way. His fleece jacket was in tatters, and both horse and rider were covered with dust. As the other racers surged forward from the starting line, their horses thundering down the valley and into the hills beyond, Kyanshay

plodded slowly after them. Soon the only other racer in sight was the beggar Grugu, prodding his ancient pony forward.

"Hail, friend," called Gesar, coming up beside him. "What a race this is when even someone like me could become king!"

"Someone like you doesn't have a chance unless half the horses go lame and the other half throw their riders," said the beggar Grugu with a sneer.

Gesar paused and looked piercingly at the beggar as he passed him. "Grugu, remember that appearances are not always what they seem." Instantly, Kyanshay sped out of sight, leaving Grugu staring open-mouthed in astonishment.

Kyanshay next approached a neatly dressed man riding sedately on an old but well cared-for horse. This was the doctor of Ling, and Gesar approached him moaning.

"What is it, man?" called the doctor.

"Doctor, I am sick. Would you stop and examine a poor man like me?"

"Yes, of course. You are Gesar, aren't you? You surely don't look like the master magician and future king of the stories I've heard about Gesar. Come here, and let me see what ails you."

Gesar dismounted and limped to the doctor's side. With a kindly smile the doctor took his wrist, then gasped in surprise.

"Gesar, in all my years, I have never felt a pulse as strong and even as yours! You are so healthy, young man, that I don't know what to say except that my prayers are with you in this race!"

Although Gesar did not reply, he was secretly satisfied to have found such a compassionate man of skill. Mounting Kyanshay once more, Gesar let him run with the wind. One by one he passed the other racers by. Few even noticed Gesar, so fast did Kyanshay move, and so intent were they on pushing their horses to the limit. Soon Gesar passed Trotun, who was whipping his horse mercilessly, in close pursuit of the leader, Lord Changpa.

Lord Changpa galloped into a ravine, and there was Gesar before him. The sight of Gesar so unnerved Changpa that he drew his horse to a halt. Glistening in silk brocade, his handsome face framed in a fine hat, Changpa was speechless in Gesar's presence.

"Changpa," Gesar said. "You are a great hero, leader of the race, leader of men. I am a poor beggar, without so much as a single friend. What a difference there is between us!"

Changpa looked carefully at Gesar. He noted Gesar's ragged, filthy clothes and his panting horse. How had this beggar come to lead the racers? Or was this a magical illusion sent by some sorcerer to deceive him?

As Changpa stared at Gesar, the beggar's form began to shimmer in front of his eyes, revealing glimpses of a noble being dressed in shining gold.

"Gesar, the old prophecies speak truly when they speak of you as our king!"

Drawing a small casket of jewels from his belt, Changpa held them out to Gesar, saying, "My eyes are no longer blind to your true form. Take this offering as a pledge of my loyalty. I had hoped to defeat Trotun and become a just king, but I now see the real King of Ling before me."

Take this as a pledge of my loyalty.

As Changpa knelt before Gesar, Lord Trotun thundered past them both. "Gesar, you must move quickly now!" Changpa said. "The evil Trotun will reach the finish line soon. If he crosses it first, he, not you, will be our rightful king and all hope for Ling will be gone."

"You need not fear for Ling, Lord Changpa. With worthy men like you to serve our kingdom, the land will prosper." Gesar commanded Kyanshay to move swiftly, and instantly Kyanshay left the ravine and was flying across the broad valley of Ling.

People tell the story of the end of the race many ways. All agree that Trotun was nearing the finish line with not another rider in sight when, like a streak of lightning, Gesar and his horse appeared. Some saw Gesar as a mighty warrior in brilliant armor riding a flame-breathing charger. Others saw only a tattered beggar astride a cloud of dust fly past Trotun to the finish line.

Everyone saw Brougmo run to Gesar's side, then joyfully lead him to the golden throne. As Gesar mounted the throne, all trace of his beggar's disguise vanished. His armor shone like the sunlight glinting on the morning dew. His smile radiated outward, filling the heart of every man and woman of Ling with hope. After many hard years the people had a king.

As each racer crossed the finish line, he dismounted and approached Gesar seated on the throne, vowing to be loyal to the new king. The last to come forward was Trotun. Full of envy and bitterness, he shouted, "The gods had decreed that I would win!"

"Lord Trotun, you have tried to harm me since I was a child. But all your evil schemes have turned to my advantage in the end. Take this jewel as a token of my thanks." Saying this, Gesar tossed him a beautiful sky-blue turquoise.

Trotun's eyes grew wide with disbelief as he recognized the turquoise he had given the raven. "I am defeated by my own trickery!" he moaned. Through clenched teeth, Trotun swore loyalty to Gesar, then slunk out of sight.

The lords of Ling joined Brougmo and Gogmo standing proudly beside Gesar. As Ling's treasures were spread before the throne, Gesar commanded, "Let these riches be used to help the people of Ling."

As the sun set on the day of the race, song and laughter filled the valley of Ling. For thirteen days and nights there was feasting and dancing. The blue sky blossomed with banners and echoed with rejoicing. Beautiful women, dressed in their finest clothes and richest jewelry, sang of the legendary heroes of Ling, while young men competed with one another in archery and horsemanship and children played their favorite games.

On the last day of celebration, the crowd grew silent as Brougmo arose from her throne. In a clear and lovely voice she told the story of how she had found Gesar and his mother, how they had captured the magical horse, and found the saddle, bridle, and armor. She finished her song with a wish for Gesar's health and happiness:

"May your life be longer than the unceasing river where waters of joy flow strong and forever. May you easily yoke the demonic hosts and convert them to truth. May I always be your inseparable companion and friend!"

In front of the people of Ling, Gesar gathered Brougmo in his arms. For Gesar and Brougmo, this was the happy beginning of a rich life and the first of many adventures that would carry them to places far beyond the Kingdom of Ling.

Let these riches be used to help the people of Ling.

King Gesar Series

For nearly a thousand years Gesar's adventures have been celebrated in Tibetan legend and song. Hundreds of versions of the Gesar epic exist, in written and spoken form. This first book of Dharma Publishing's King Gesar Series is the latest retelling of the story of Gesar's birth and the great horse race. Later books will take us with Gesar and Brougmo on courageous journeys to the wild lands and evil kingdoms on the borders of Ling.

The origin of the Gesar epic can be traced through historical records to the eleventh century when a king named Gesar ruled the kingdom of Ling in an area of high peaks and deep river valleys near the Amnye Machin mountains.

Gesar's heroic task is to overcome the dark forces, both inner and outer, that bring war and hardship and obscure the path to enlightenment. Each character in the epic, from the evil Lord Trotun to the celestial beings that guide Gesar in his quest, symbolizes a psychological and spiritual force. Gesar harnesses and unifies these forces, just as he unifies the kingdom of Ling. Gesar's ultimate victory promises that peace, harmony, and enlightenment will prevail in the world.

Pronunciation guide: The sound of Tibetan words can be difficult to express in English spelling. Even in Tibet, pronunciation varies from region to region, and there can be several ways to sound out the same word. These general guidelines will help you pronounce the names in this story. Gesar: *Ge* rhymes with *say*, *sar* rhymes with *far*. Brougmo: *Brou* is pronounced *drew*, and *mo* is pronounced *mow*, so Brougmo really sounds more like *drewk-mow*. Gogmo combines the sounds *go*, *oak*, and *mow*, and is pronounced *goak-mow*. Kyanshay: *kyan* sounds like *key on* and *shay* rhymes with *day*. Trotun: *Tro* rhymes with *row*, and *tun* sounds like *ton*.

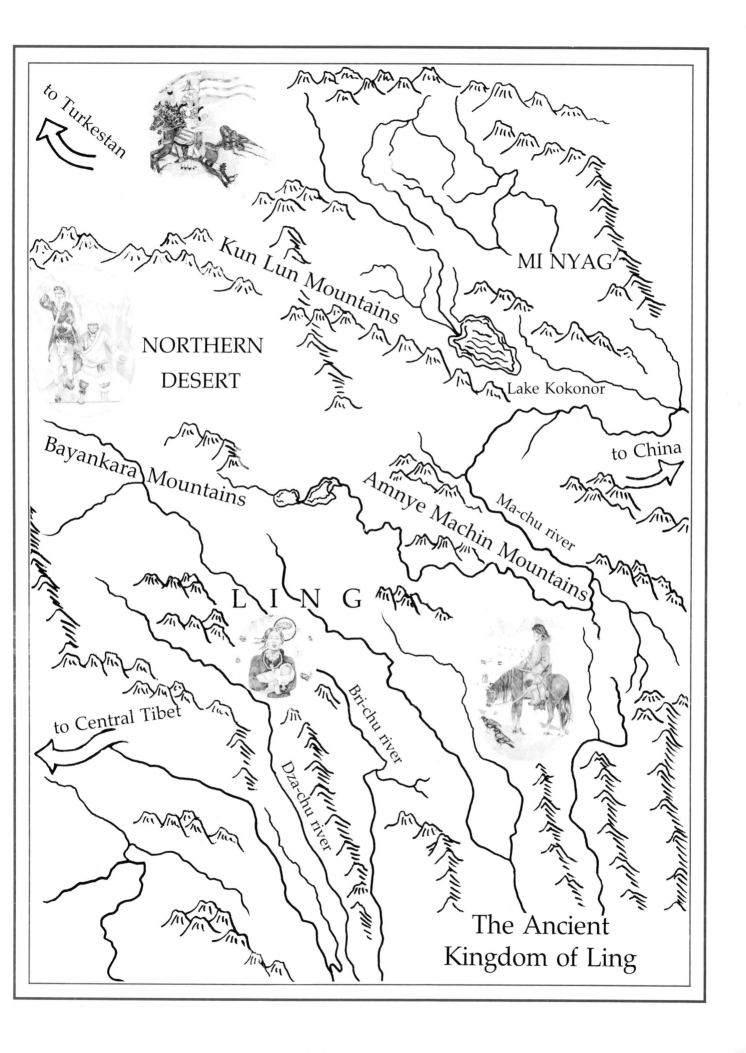

to Turkestan

Kun Lun Mountains

NORTHERN
DESERT

Bayankara Mountains

MI NYAG

Lake Kokonor

to China

Amnye Machin Mountains

Ma-chu river

L I N G

to Central Tibet

Bri-chu river

Dza-chu river

The Ancient
Kingdom of Ling